THE CASE OF THE PUPPY ACADEMY

THE SAMANTHA RAIN MYSTERIES 2.5

ARIZONA TAPE

BLURB

Even hellhounds need training.

When Samantha Rain takes her hellhound to school, she hoped to be surrounded by adorable magical puppies. Instead, she finds herself at the heart of a mystery and she's forced to investigate a jewellery thief. With all the important people at the Puppy Academy, she can't afford to step on any toes… or paws.

-

The Case Of The Puppy Academy is a bonus story in the Samantha Rain Mysteries and happens between The Night Mark and The Pixie Deal.

CHAPTER ONE

EVEN HELLHOUNDS NEEDED TRAINING. Six hours of puppy school and according to the brochure Samantha was holding, there would be mandatory assessments on the bond between her and her puppy.

With her recently-adopted hellhound on the lead, she entered the Puppy Academy through automatic sliding doors and made her way to the front desk.

"Welcome to the Puppy Academy," the sleek receptionist greeted. "What can I do for you?"

"I'm here for the beginner's puppy course."

The woman nodded, her shiny hair cascading down her shoulders. "Name?"

"Samantha Rain."

"Samantha… Rain…" she repeated. She looked up

from the computer screen, her big eyes framed with gold glitter. "Species?"

"Shadow is a hellhound, but I don't know what breed," Sam replied, staring down at the puppy. With her silver colours, she could easily be mistaken for a normal, grey dog that had nothing to do with the supernatural. Until the glowing blue patterns came out. Then it was a little harder to explain.

The secretary chuckled. "No, honey. *Your* species."

"Oh. Right." A blush crept up Sam's neck. Even after being part of the secret Nocturnal world for a month, she still wasn't used to having to clarify that. "Human."

"Perfect…" The keys of her old computer clacked loudly. "And your alliance?"

"Clan IF. The Will-o-Wisps?"

"I know Clan IF." The secretary held out her arm, blinding Samantha with a polished silver bracelet that held the emblem of the IF family. "Your hellhound looks to be the blue wisp breed."

"Okay, is that good?" She really wished she had more information about her own dog, but the adoption had happened so quickly and she couldn't exactly use the internet for this.

The woman shrugged. "Blue wisps are inquisitive, friendly, and they have a great sense of smell."

"They do?" Sam bent down to give Shadow a scratch between her ears. "You got a good nose? You got a good nose?"

The puppy sat down and stared curiously at Sam.

While she knew the dog couldn't understand her, it didn't stop her from talking to Shadow in a baby voice. "You'll learn."

With a chuckle, she returned to the conversation with the receptionist. "Is everything alright? My, ummm... Lilith said she enrolled me."

"Just confirming your attendance. You're all set." With an aggressive tap, she finished the form and gestured to a set of large swinging doors. "Class starts in fifteen minutes, just go through the doors on your right, your course is at the end of the hall."

"Thank you." Samantha tugged on the lead, egging Shadow in motion.

The small puppy yawned and waggled behind Samantha. Both had no idea what to expect from their first class, but the Puppy Academy was the best school in the city to train a hellhound.

CHAPTER TWO

IT WASN'T until Samantha and Shadow passed through the swinging doors that they realised just how soundproof the reception was. As soon as they stepped into the hallway, they could hear multiple dogs. Some were whining, others barking, and there was even a howl or two in the mix.

"Awrooo!" Shadow replied, bouncing up and down. She hadn't been in the company of other dogs, supernatural or not, and the prospect of playing with them seemed to excite her.

Samantha steadied the lead and pulled the hellhound puppy away from one of the doors. A thin window revealed a chaotic playroom with at least ten or twenty other dogs chasing a ball. Sam needed a double-take to realise they were all different from regular dogs. Some had glowing patterns on their fur or flames around their legs. Others even had electricity crackling down their tails.

Despite their supernatural nature, they were all acting like dogs and from the looks of it, Shadow seemed all too eager to join them. She scratched at the door and pressed her wet nose against the glass, trying to make friends.

"No." Sam tugged on the lead. "Come away."

Shadow didn't listen, but Samantha didn't blame her. That was why they came to the Academy in the first place, to train.

She gently pulled on the lead again and managed to tease her away from the crowded playroom. A smile tugged on her lips and with the affectionate feelings growing in her chest, she scratched the puppy on her head. "Good girl."

"Wraf!" The usually tight lead relaxed as the puppy bounced around Samantha's feet, her full attention back to her owner. "Wraf?"

"Yes, yes, you can get a treat." Sam patted her pockets, trying to remember where she put the pouch of snacks. The sound of crinkling plastic made Shadow dance in excitement and it wasn't long before she managed to wrap Sam's legs with the lead.

"Shadow! Careful." She pulled the treats from her

jacket and the mere presence of snacks made the puppy sit down.

She wagged her tail a million miles per hour and whined until Samantha dropped a couple of treats down. Within a second, they were hoovered up and Shadow was already begging for more.

"That's it for now." Despite the way it tugged on her heart, Sam ignored the adorable look she got from the hellhound and pocketed the treats. "Come on. Come on."

Shadow's tongue dangled out of her mouth as she jumped around. She seemed happy to follow Sam, especially now that she knew there were treats.

"Good girl," Sam encouraged. The two ventured further into the hallway, away from the distracting playpen. The further they got, the less Shadow tugged on her lead. She was just happy to follow along.

Just as Samantha thought she had everything under control and that training was going to be a breeze, her puppy charged straight ahead.

"Wraf! Wraf! Wraf!!" Shadow barked at the wall. She struggled against the tensed lead, trying to get closer to the corner. "Wraf!"

"Hey, hey! What's that about?"

Sam tried to pull the puppy away, but Shadow wouldn't listen. She pressed her nose into the dusty

7

corner and as she growled, the patterns hidden under her fur glowed their signature blue.

"Shadow! Stop. Come away," Sam tried again, but to no avail. To make matters worse, the swinging doors clappered loudly and another person stepped into the hallway.

Slender and tall, he had his own puppy on the lead who was a lot better behaved than Shadow. The reddish dog completely ignored the room of playing dogs and stayed attached to the man's heel as he walked back to Samantha.

Samantha pulled on the lead again, drawing the hellhound away from the corner. The presence of another dog was far more interesting and the two puppies were quickly sniffing each other's behind.

"Everything alright?" The man asked, gesturing at Shadow.

Embarrassment crept up to her cheeks that someone saw how little control she had over her dog. "Yes, everything is fine."

"Are you here for the puppy training class?" he asked, a bemused smile playing on his lips as she watched the two dogs darting around each other.

"I am. You?" Sam kept a close eye on the puppies, concerned about Shadow's reaction. She'd never played with another dog before and the red puppy was a lot bigger than hers.

"Same," the man replied. With a simple click of his tongue, his dog abandoned the introduction and returned to his heel.

"Impressive," Sam noted. "If she listens so well, why are you here?"

"He. And hellhound training is mandatory."

"Oh, right."

He gestured to the classroom. "Shall we?"

"Yes, of course." She tugged on Shadow's lead, urging her in the right direction. "Here, girl."

"I'm Aaron," the man said, holding out his hand. He gestured to his puppy. "And this is Tomato, but we call him Tommy."

Samantha memorised his features and quickly shook his hand. "Nice to meet you, Aaron. Samantha and Shadow."

"I assume Shadow is the dog?" he joked.

"Yes, of course." She pulled on the lead again. "Here girl."

"Wraf!" The novelty of the other dog had worn off and Shadow returned to barking at the corner. "Wraf!"

"There's nothing there!" Sam protested. "What are you looking at?"

"Maybe a ghost?"

Aaron's suggestion made Sam shiver. "A ghost? You're kidding, right?"

After meeting Vampires, Will-O-Wisps, and what not, she was prepared for anything. The Nox world was filled with mysterious creatures, she just hoped ghosts weren't part of it.

He shot her an amused smile. "Yes, I'm kidding... Or am I?"

CHAPTER THREE

To Samantha's surprise, there were more people in the puppy class than she expected. She counted seven others, besides herself, Aaron, and the teacher. That was a lot of people in the know about the secret world of the Nox.

At least, she guessed all the other participants were humans like her. From what she'd been told, the Nox almost never took ownership over a familiar. Most Wardens were human.

From the look of the group, Samantha differentiated at least three other breeds of hellhounds. A black puppy sat near the window, while two golden-coated ones were running around their owner's legs. A couple of reddish ones were playing together in the corner, barking and growling away. One of them bit the other in the tail and just like that, he burst into flames.

"Aaah! Your dog is on fire!" Sam shrieked, earning a couple of confused looks. It took her a moment to realise this was probably normal and that the puppy wasn't bothered. "Nevermind."

She turned away, facing a chuckling Aaron.

"What's so funny?" She glared at him. "I thought the puppy was hurt."

"I had the exact same reaction when Tommy combusted for the first time. He almost set my house on fire too."

"Oh." That made her feel a little less foolish. "What breed is he?"

"I believe they call it a red blaze. I think it's fairly obvious why."

"Fairly," Samantha muttered. She'd never expected there to be so many different kinds of hell-hounds. How they all stayed hidden from the human world was a miracle.

She watched Shadow chase her tail until the teacher called everyone's attention for the first lesson of the day.

"I'm Carla, Penny's trainer." She patted her thigh and addressed the big dog in the back of the room. "Come here, girl!"

A yellow hound trotted between the playful

puppies, not even batting an eye as she passed the yipping balls of fluff. Some of them were so exhausted, they were yawning.

"Sit, Penny," the trainer instructed and obediently, the big dog thudded down next to her owner. "Good girl."

"Impressive," I muttered, staring at Shadow who was chewing on her own tail. She still had a long way to go.

Carla held up a bag of treats, immediately gaining the attention of Penny and some of the other puppies. "Here at puppy school, we like to work with positive enforcement. You tell them the command and when they do it, whether by accident or skill, you reward them with a little treat. Like so."

She pointed to the floor. "Down."

Penny immediately laid on her stomach and looked up expectantly. She seemed especially pleased when the trainer held out a piece of dog candy and lapped it up without hesitation. She tipped her head to the side and sniffed the bag of treats, eager for more.

"Wait," Carla instructed.

With a whine, Penny laid her head down on her stretched out legs. She never took her eye off the treats though.

Next to me, Aaron chuckled. "That dog is so well behaved."

"Very," Samantha agreed. "Shadow never listens to me. She just likes to follow me around the house and play with my shoes."

"Tommy carries my socks. I suppose we're here to learn."

She looked hesitantly at her own puppy, who had given up chasing her own tail and was now running as far as her lead allowed. Her little puppy legs carried her as fast as they could, straight into a wall.

Sam grimaced. "Ouch. I suppose so. Shadow! Come here. Come."

The puppy perked up from hearing her name, shot her owner a questioning glance, and ran the opposite direction.

"Noooo. Shadow, come here. Sit. Sit!"

"Ahem." Trainer Carla crossed the room towards Samantha and gestured to the two of them. "Having some trouble?"

"A little," Sam admitted.

"What's her name?"

"Shadow."

Carla nodded and crouched down to the puppy's level. "Shadow. Here, girl. Come, come, come."

The excitement in her voice drew Shadow

towards her and the puppy bounced right into her arms.

"Good girl!" The trainer turned back to Samantha. "Did you bring some treats?"

"Yes, of course." She patted her pockets again for the bag. "Here."

"Give her one. Associate good behaviour with rewards and in time, she'll learn to associate the name with herself and that it's nice to come when she's being called."

Samantha nodded. That made a lot of sense and she didn't know why she hadn't come up with that herself. She pulled one of the treats from the bag and dropped it next to Shadow's paw.

"Ah, it's better to feed it from your hand when you're training," Carla corrected. She gestured to Sam's bag. "Can I?"

"Yes, sure." She handed the treats to the trainer and watched her handle the enthusiastic puppy with more success than she'd had.

Shadow jumped up against Carla's legs, but a firm no got her quickly back on all fours.

"Sit," the trainer commanded and as soon as the puppy responded, she gave her another treat. She repeated it until Shadow understood that if she sat down, she got snacks. That seemed like music to her puppy ears.

Samantha watched the entire exchange in surprise. It was incredible to see her puppy behave after just a couple of minutes with someone that knew what they were doing. Back at home, she'd tried some tips she found on the internet, but she never managed to keep Shadow's attention for long enough.

Carla handed her the treats back and smiled encouragingly. "Blue wisps are very intelligent breeds. With regular exercise, you'll have her trained in no time."

"Thank you," Samantha smiled. She pointed at her shoes and tried to mimic the tone of the trainer. "Shadow, sit."

Eager to please and desperate for treats, the puppy quickly sat down and licked her lips as she looked at the bag with goodies.

To reward her good behaviour, Sam quickly handed her one. "Good girl."

"Excellent," Carla complimented. "I hope everyone watched that exchange. Most dogs are eager to please their owner, so together with treats, give them verbal and physical encouragement. Use a light tone of voice to tell them they did well and pet their heads. Don't shout or hit them. We *never* use punishment to train our companions. Never. Is that understood?"

"Yes," Samantha said in unison with the rest of the other Wardens. It wasn't a hard promise. Just looking at Shadow made her melt. With her adorable floppy ears and her big, begging eyes, the puppy was the cutest thing she'd ever seen. She couldn't imagine hitting or hurting her dog and she didn't understand how some people could be so cruel either.

If anyone dared harm Shadow, she wasn't confident she'd be able to obey the very same law she used to work so hard to uphold. There would be retribution if someone hurt her puppy.

Sam's eyes widened from her own thoughts. She'd always abided by the law and held it in the highest regard. That was why she became a detective in the first place, to catch people who didn't think the rules applied to them.

Maybe she'd been spending so much time in the hidden Nox world that it had started to alter her sense of right and wrong. From everything she'd seen, the Nocturnal clans seemed to thrive on operating outside the law and bending the rules.

Not exactly something Sam could condone, but there was nothing she could do about it.

"Shadow, sit," she commanded, pleased when the puppy listened. She reached down to give her a little treat and in return, the puppy licked her hand.

Whether it was to give her kisses or search for more treats, Samantha didn't know. She didn't care either. There was something soothing about the softness of a dog's tongue and the affectionate lapping.

She ruffled Shadow's ears, remembering that vocal affirmation was key to the training. "Good girl. You're such a good girl, aren't you? Yes, you are. Yes, you are!"

With the puppy's full attention on her, they practised the same command until Shadow got bored and wandered off to play with Tommy.

She clonked him on the head, but he just shrugged it off and sniffed her.

"They're cute together," Aaron sat, gesturing to the two dogs chasing each other's tail.

Samantha smiled. "Very. There's nothing like a room full of puppies. I always wanted one."

"How come you waited?"

A bittersweet sensation drove her smile away. "My partner didn't like dogs."

"But your husband came around?"

A lump formed in Samantha's throat, but she shook it away. "Wife. And no, she didn't come around. We split up."

"Oh, sorry to hear that." The man shot her a sympathetic smile. "At least you don't have to hide the Nox from her then?"

"I suppose not… Is that what you're doing?"

Aaron's smile evaporated. "I have to. I have a little girl who needs her father. I can't afford to be banished from the Gravitas. Or worse…"

"You're allied with the Gravitas family?" Sam asked in surprise. "But you seem so…"

"Normal? Neutral?" He chuckled. "Isn't that our job as Wardens?"

"I suppose so…" She gestured to the other people in the room. "I guess this is a great place for us to get to know the other Wardens of the city. I'm sure in time, we'll be running into each other as ambassadors of our clans."

Aaron nodded. "Exactly. My Master says this is a great exercise in diplomacy, since we're the only ones allowed to travel across all the Nox territories."

"Hmmm, true…"

It was all a bit much for Sam. It was one thing to find out a secret, supernatural world was hidden right beneath humanity's nose. It was a completely different thing to become part of that world. Adopting a hellhound had made her a Warden and now she was bound by the Law of Six, the only rules that the Nox listened to. At least, when it was convenient for them. When they stirred up trouble, it was the family Wardens that needed to resolve the conflicts.

Samantha bent down to kiss Shadow's snout. "You're lucky you're so cute."

Otherwise, she would've walked away from the Nocturnal world.

CHAPTER FOUR

AFTER AN HOUR OF RIGOROUS TRAINING, which involved a lot of tail-wagging, treat-eating, and begging puppy-eyes, the class came to their first break.

"That's it for the morning. Please leave the puppies here so I can conduct the first assessment on their characters. There's tea and coffee in the cafeteria, and you can get something to eat as well."

"We have to leave our dogs?" Sam asked, reluctant to leave Shadow alone with all the other puppies. She didn't know them, but from the looks of it, one of the blaze hellhounds seemed pretty aggressive.

Carla nodded. "Yes, but they'll be supervised the entire time. Don't worry. Class will resume after lunch."

"Alright…" Samantha bowed down to give Shadow a couple of pets and unclicked the lead. "Behave, okay?"

"Awrr?" Shadow tipped her head to the side so far she fell over.

"You're so silly." She kissed the puppy on her head. "I'll be back soon. Be a good girl."

Reluctantly, Samantha walked out with Aaron. She didn't like leaving Shadow somewhere strange, but she didn't have another choice.

On her way to the cafeteria, a familiar figure awaited her.

"Lilith?" Sam said, subconsciously pushing her hair behind her ear. "W-What are you doing here?"

Lilith shot her a signature pearly smile. "I came to see how you and Demon Bite were doing."

"Her name is Shadow, but that's… sweet." She studied the beautiful woman carefully. "And suspicious?"

"Why? Can't I be thoughtful?" Lilith held out her hand to greet Sam's new associate. "I'm Lilith, Samantha's partner. And you are?"

"Aaron, Gravitas Warden," the man introduced. He turned back to Samantha, a frown weaved between his thin eyebrows. "I thought you said your wife didn't like dogs?"

Sam's cheeks flushed red. "Oh, god, no. Lilith is not that kind of a partner. She's my…"

"Boss," Lilith finished her sentence. "Technically. Hi, I'm Lilith Fatuus. I'm—"

"You're the IF heir," Aaron said, the surprise clear on his face. "What are you doing here?"

"I happen to love dogs." Lilith shot Samantha another smile. "Lunch?"

A little flabbergasted, Sam gestured to the cafeteria sign hanging above the door. "We were just heading there."

"Hmmm… I don't think so." The woman pulled up her nose at the thought of eating cheap, mass-produced food. "There's a lovely little café across the street. Have lunch with me there."

A new blush crept up Samantha's neck. "That sounds nice, but I don't want to leave Shadow alone for too long…"

"Fine…" Lilith rolled her eyes dramatically as only she could. With ease, she synched her pace with Sam's, her heels clicking loudly on the stone floor. "Cafeteria it is. But if you try to make me eat a sausage roll, we're done."

"Alright, no sausages for you." Despite herself, Samantha chuckled. There was something about the younger woman that kept her on her toes. Everything and anything else disappeared, just like always.

She even forgot about Aaron and didn't notice him breaking away and joining another group of Wardens. She was too fixated on Lilith.

A mischievous twinkle passed through the other woman's silver eyes. "At least, not when I'm with you."

"You're incorrigible."

"And you love that," she teased. "Oh my, it smells like cafeteria."

"I wonder why that is."

"Oh no..." Lilith picked a tray using just two fingers and stared at it as if she'd never seen anything so insulting. "I don't think I can do this."

Sam chuckled lightly. She had to admit that the Nox woman looked entirely out of place in the shabby cafeteria. Between everyone's comfortable clothes and the staff's hairnets, Lilith's expensive dress and high heels stood out like a crown on a pig.

She'd never seen Lilith in anything but an immaculate get-up, which seemed like a lot of wasted effort to her. Samantha certainly didn't care for all the make-up and eyeliner. Perhaps that was her age, but she just couldn't bother spending hours in front of a mirror. With her looks, it would just end up depressing her.

Then again... she wasn't nearly as young, beautiful, or radiant as Lilith. If she had the woman's high cheekbones or sparkling eyes, maybe she'd want to draw attention to them too.

They queued with the other Wardens, using the metal rails to slide the tray along. A regular feat for Sam, an absolute horror for Lilith.

"What's that tub of yellow mush?" Lilith asked, gesturing ahead. "Don't tell me that's mashed potatoes."

Sam snorted. "You sound so appalled."

"I am. Don't tell me this is normal."

"It's pretty standard for a big kitchen."

"I think you'll find standard is exactly what they're lacking here." Lilith flinched when they refilled the beef stew tub and pulled up her nose. "Oh, I don't think so."

"Just get a burger or some salad. It's perfectly fine." Samantha nodded as the server held up a ladle of stew. "Yes, please. Can I have rice with that?"

Lilith rejected any of the server's offers and gestured to the heaping pile of brown sludge on Sam's plate. "You're seriously going to eat that?"

"It smells good," Samantha shrugged. "I've been eating freezer meals since my wife left me. This is heaven."

"How sad..." The other woman reluctantly agreed to a scoop of vegetables and a piece of fish.

"You need to go out more, Samantha. Meet someone in a bar, or even try swiping."

"Right… And what's the point of getting to know someone, only so I can hide the Nox world from them?" After passing through the till, she selected a table near the window and sat down opposite of the other woman. "I'll pass on dating."

Lilith shrugged. "There are plenty of humans aware of our world."

"You're telling me I should date another Warden?" Sam didn't know why, but Lilith's suggestion hurt.

"Why not? Statistically, there must be other lesbian Wardens." She stuck her fork in a green bean and grimaced as it spurted juice all over the table. "This can't be legal."

"You're overreacting," Sam sighed. She pushed her plate away, her appetite suddenly gone.

"You're not eating either."

"I'm not hungry anymore. Can we just stop talking about my love life, or the lack of it?"

Lilith threw her napkin in her plate. "Sure. How's Demon Bite doing?"

"Shadow. And Good."

"Good? That's it?"

"Yes." Sam checked the time on her watch and gestured over her shoulder. "You know, I should get back to class. I want to make sure my hellhound is alright."

"O-Okay."

Hurt flashed over Lilith's face, but it happened so fast, Samantha wasn't sure she saw it right. When the Nox woman rose from her seat, any hint of vulnerability was long gone.

She smoothed out her black dress and threw her hair over her shoulder. "I should get back too. This is not really my scene anyway."

"Clearly," Samantha muttered as she picked up her tray. "Aren't you going to take yours?"

"And do what with it?"

"Put it on the food cart?"

Lilith scoffed haughtily. "Please…"

She shot the tray a dismissive glare and without looking back once, she strode away.

"Hey!" Samantha called, but it was no use and she knew it. When Lilith got something in her head, nobody was going to change that.

She collected the two plates and returned the trays to the food carts. She knew she'd be hungry later, but she had a lasagna in the freezer that would have to scratch that itch. Dinner for one, just as always.

CHAPTER FIVE

"You're early." Trainer Carla looked up from her clipboard and waved Samantha in. "Everything alright?"

"Yes, I was just missing Shadow," she replied. Not a complete lie, but it wasn't the entire truth either, Samantha thought.

"The blue wisp, right?" The trainer flipped through her assessment pages. "Since you're early, we can discuss my evaluation, if you'd like."

"Sure." Samantha scanned the room for the puppies, searching for hers. Between the extroverted sparking hellhounds and brazen blaze breed, it seemed her dog was more on the shy side. "Shadow?"

"Awrr!" A silver ball of fluff broke free from the group and darted towards Sam. "Awrr!"

"Hey, puppy. How are you? How are you? Were you a good girl? Were you?"

Carla chuckled. "She was. She played well with the others."

"Aww, did you?" Sam coed, fluffing Shadow's ears. "Good job, Shadow. Yes, good job."

"She also reacted well to foreign toys and she showed a lot of courage when we tried the tunnel. She's a clever one, and very eager to please. It's still early days, but she shows great promise to become a working dog. I think you should consider our advanced puppy course."

"Oh, really?" Samantha beamed with pride. "You think so?"

"She might be too timid for guarding or attacking, but she'd be excellent at tracking and fetching. As a Warden, you could benefit from the extra security from having your hellhound by your side. Especially when dealing with some of the… less pleasant parts of our job. We might be protected by the Law of Six, but there are plenty of Nox that don't respect Wardens from their own clan, let alone other clans."

"I used to be a detective, I'm perfectly capable of dealing with those things." She looked down at the playful puppy and thought about Lilith. It was highly unusual for a Nox of her standing to accompany her so often on her Warden duties. She probably wouldn't keep that up, especially not if Sam couldn't make up her mind what was going on between the two of them.

"But it might be nice to be able to take Shadow along during work," she concluded. She gave Shadow a little scratch between her ears and earned a happy yip. "Good girl."

The puppy bounced around her feet, not any less exhausted than when Samantha left her. She drummed her paws on the floor, challenging Sam to play with her.

"Such a ball of energy, you are." She waved her hand in front of Shadow's snout in a teasing hand game. While the puppy was distracted by her dancing fingers, she turned back to talk to Carla. "Is there anything else I should know about her?"

"She's very inquisitive and treat-motivated. Are you home a lot?"

"Umm... I'm gone during the day, but I'm usually home in the evening. Depends on what case I'm working."

"Case?"

"I investigate murders, thefts, disappearances. It's not as official as when I used to be part of the force, but my orders come directly from the heir, so... I suppose it's not that different."

The trainer nodded. "I see. You're part of clan IF,

correct?"

"Yes. How did you know?"

"Ah, they're the only family that breeds blue wisps in town. If you're part of that clan, you must know Lilith Fatuus?"

"I do, yes."

"Hmmm… Some advice, Warden to Warden… You should be careful with her."

Samantha frowned. "Excuse me?"

"She's got a widespread reputation for being manipulative, twisted, and very aggressive. I'd avoid her as much as possible, if I were you."

Despite her argument with Lilith, Samantha's scowled. "I don't care for gossip. Not that it's any of your business, but Lilith is a friend. Why don't you stick to what you know? Hounds."

Carla's face fell as soon as she realised she made a mistake. "My apologies, I shouldn't have said anything."

"No, you shouldn't have. What clan are you from?"

"Gravitas."

Samantha nodded. "What branch?"

"C…"

"I see. Your Master, Catalina, owes me a favour or two." She stared at the other woman in disgust. She didn't often utter threats, but when it came to her friends or family, she would do anything to protect them. Regardless of how she became part of the clan, she was treated well by Lilith and after being discharged from the police and her recent, ongoing divorce, it had given her a new purpose. "I think it's best you don't spread any more rumours about Clan IF or Lilith, don't you think? It would be a shame if I had to complain to Catalina about you."

The trainer bowed her head in shame as she backed away. "Of course, I apologise."

Samantha wanted nothing more than to leave the Puppy Academy, but she knew she couldn't. She needed to train her puppy and she couldn't take Shadow to a regular dog school without exposing the Nox world. She had no choice but to stay.

She focused her attention on Shadow, finding comfort in the puppy's playful nature. This puppy deserved the best training she could get, even if that came from a judgmental person. There was no denying Carla was good at handling the hellhounds and she'd just have to put up with her.

She turned away, only to find Lilith standing in the doorway. Her appearance startled the trainer, who shot a desperate look at Sam.

Samantha's lips curled into a grin. "Speak of the devil."

"And she shall appear," Lilith finished. She click-clacked her way into the room with a confidence that Sam envied. She just did it so gracefully and elegant, it was impossible to take her eyes off of her.

She swallowed audibly. "Why are you back?"

"I need to talk to you. Alone."

"Oh, alright." Samantha turned to the trainer. She didn't like bossing people around, but the situation called for it. "Make sure nothing happens to Shadow."

"Y-Yes, of course," Carla stammered.

The two women strode away, leaving her flustered with a cluster of dogs that never seemed to tire. Whether that was due to their hellhound nature or just the fact that they were puppies, she didn't know.

In the hallway, Samantha and Lilith paused a little away from the playpen. As soon as they were sure they were alone, Lilith's smile disappeared.

"What's wrong?" Sam asked. She couldn't explain why, but seeing Lilith frown upset her. It wasn't normal for the woman to be torn up and she hated to think what made her feel this way.

Lilith held up her hand and wiggled her finger. "This."

"What?"

"I'm missing my ring. My clan ring," she hissed, checking over her shoulder to make sure nobody could overhear them. "It's a family heirloom, my father would kill me if he found out I lost it."

"What? How did you lose it?" She grabbed Lilith's hand and pulled it closer, as if that somehow would help with finding the ring.

"I don't know! Someone must've lifted it. Oh, if I find that person, I'll kill them." Lilith trembled with seething anger and Samantha felt sorry for whoever dared steal from the will-o-wisp heir. While 'heir' sounded all eloquent and fancy, the clan wasn't run like a monarchy. It was a mob and Lilith would soon be the big Boss.

Being merciful wasn't part of her job description.

Samantha ran her hand through her short hair. "Maybe you just lost it? Did you take it off to wash your hands?"

"I never take it off."

"You should. It's better for your skin."

Lilith's eyes flashed angrily. "I would rather cut my hand off than take the ring off my finger."

"Woah, alright, alright. So you didn't take it off." Samantha held up her hands, hoping for peace. "But honestly... Who could've been so stupid to steal your clan ring?"

"Good question." The Nox woman's eyes returned to their normal bright blue, but they sparkled with menace. "Who indeed."

CHAPTER SIX

LILITH WAS FUMING like an overworked steam train. "I'll stop at nothing until I find my ring. I'll turn this entire academy upside down and all the people in it too. Anyone could be the thief."

"You shouldn't just start accusing people," Samantha said. "They're all Wardens from powerful families. They will not take kindly to a false accusation. No, this has to stay between us and the thief."

"Sam..." Lilith growled.

"No. You assigned me as one of your advisors, so take my advice. No rushing into things. Your... brazen approach might make you enemies and you can't afford to start a turf war. Especially not you"

"What's that supposed to mean?"

Samantha pulled a face. "You don't have the greatest reputation..."

"What? What did you hear?"

"That you're manipulative and aggressive."

"Me? Aggressive?" Lilith yelled, startling a couple of Wardens passing them in the hallway on their return to the puppy room. After seeing their shocked faces, the Nox woman conceded. "Fine... What do you suggest?"

"I'll talk to some people, ask around about time schedules, establish the most likely suspects. Let me do what I do best."

"Fine. But if you haven't figured it out by the end of the day, I'll torture anyone that had access to the place."

"Give me at least two days," Samantha countered. "And no torturing."

"One day. And what about a light whipping?"

"One day, no whipping." She gave Lilith her most determined look, hoping she hadn't lost her barter skills.

For a moment, it looked like the other woman wasn't going to bite, but then she reached out to shake Sam's hand. "Deal."

"Deal," Samantha replied, ignoring the softness of Lilith's palm. This was not the time nor the place. She quickly pulled her arm back and shoved her hands deep in her pockets. "Now I have to get back to class. We're going to teach the puppies another command. But. I'll try and gather some information, hmm?"

"Alright... I could stay, maybe ask some questions, intimidate some people—"

"No, I think it's best you leave. I'll brief you on my findings when I leave."

"Oh, I'm not leaving."

"Please..." Sam reached across to gently touch Lilith's arm. Despite herself, she couldn't resist the urge to comfort the younger woman. "I'll get your ring back. You can count on me."

Lilith's eyes softened and she nodded. "Okay. But I'm picking you up after your classes."

"Alright, but now I have to go, the new session is about to start."

"Go, go," the Nox encouraged her. "I'll see you later."

"You promise to go away and not grill everyone you see?"

Lilith ground her teeth together. "Fine... After I retrace my steps and search every inch of this place."

Sam threw her hands up. She knew when to fight and when a battle was lost. "Fine."

She rejoined the rest of the Wardens for their second class of the day, hoping that she could find a way to defuse the situation. If she couldn't find this ring, Lilith would bring chaos into the academy, and she'd be in no position to stop her. A tornado didn't change their path of destruction for anyone and the same was true for Lilith.

Sam was just pleased she managed to stall her.

"Hey." Aaron waved at her from the back of the room.

"Hi."

With Shadow dancing around her legs, she joined the slender man near the window. "Did I miss anything?"

"No, trainer Carla just showed a couple of tricks." He clicked his tongue to draw one of the red hellhounds closer. "Tommy, here boy."

The blaze puppy's ears immediately perked up and without hesitation, he dropped his toy and waddled over to his owner.

"He's so well behaved," Sam complimented. "How did you do that at home?"

"I grew up training dogs."

"But you still have to come to the Puppy Academy?"

Aaron sighed. "Yes. It's mandatory."

"This must be boring for you then."

"A little. But I look forward to the advanced blaze classes. My Master prefers if his Wardens have a trained hellhound by their side."

"Ah, I see. What branch are you from?"

"A, like my name suggests."

Samantha frowned. "I know the Gravitas are strict about how they name their members, but I didn't realise that extended to the Wardens."

"It does."

"How does that work? What if you're marked but your name doesn't start with the right letter?"

Aaron let out a long breath. "You change your name."

"Really? That's... something," she muttered, deciding it was best not to find a name for that practice. "What if you don't want to?"

"That's not an option."

"Oh." Samantha pulled a face. She'd never been more grateful to be part of Clan IF and be under Lilith's protection. While her life had changed now she was aware of the Nox, it wasn't that different than before. The biggest difference hadn't come from Lilith's appearance. They'd been caused by her separation and that had nothing to do with the Nox.

"There's a saying in our clan. Choose a new name or have your old one carved in your tombstone.'" Aaron made a finger gun and pointed it at Tommy. "Bang."

The puppy tilted his head to the side before rolling onto his back. While holding perfectly still, he opened one eye and looked at his owner.

"Good boy," he praised. He looked back at Samantha with a broad smile, but he didn't manage to hide the pain in his eyes. "Don't listen to me. I was honoured to become part of Gravitas."

"Right..."

"I was. I was chosen." He reached down to play with Tommy's ears. "It's better this way."

Samantha decided it was best to abandon the sensitive conversation and focus on Shadow instead. Despite all the playtime, she still wasn't tired and the bounciness wasn't helping with learning the right commands.

She gestured at the ground. "Sit."

The puppy just tilted her head to the side and wagged her tail.

"Sit. Shadow, sit?"

"Arf!" She shimmered an excited blue and jumped around Sam's feet, not tired in the slightest.

"We'll try again at home." She checked her watch and cringed as she saw the time. She really needed to start questioning people if she was going to find Lilith's ring. She just wasn't sure where to start. The other Wardens? The trainer? The receptionist?

She dropped a treat for her hellhound and decided to talk to Carla first. It seemed unlikely that she had time to leave the puppies alone to steal Lilith's ring, so she was a good neutral starting point.

"Hey, Carla?" Samantha approached the other woman. "Could I have a word?"

"Of course." The trainer rounded her conversation with another Warden and joined Sam in the corner. "Listen, about before—"

"Don't mention it. It's water under the bridge."

Carla let out a visible sigh of relief. "Oof. Okay, thanks. So, what can I do for you?"

"Do you like working at the Puppy Academy?"

She seemed taken aback by Sam's question. "Umm... I guess so."

"It's just such a fascinating concept to me. Wardens from all clans coming together to train their hellhounds. Are there no conflicts?"

"Well, any place has conflicts, but not the sort you're referring to. We're all part of a clan, but ultimately, our job as Wardens is to keep the fragile peace. That wouldn't happen if we refused to work together."

Samantha nodded. "I suppose so, yes. Are all the teachers and staff Wardens too? Or is the facility run by Nox?"

"Both. Are you interested in applying for a position?"

"Oh. Yes," Sam lied. She wasn't, but that would make the trainer less suspicious. "Is it a nice place to work?"

"Yes, very. I enjoy it."

"That's good to hear. My last workplace was rather…" She thought back to her police department and the way she got passed over. "Toxic. Rude comments, discrimination, you couldn't leave valuables in your locker. That sort of thing doesn't happen here, does it?"

"Oh no, absolutely not."

"Hmmm." Samantha realised her disappointed hum probably didn't make sense, so she quickly covered it up with a smile. "That's reassuring. I'll think it over again."

"If you have any more questions…"

"No, not right now. Thank you." She returned to the back of the room, processing everything the trainer told her. If she'd been able to question her more aggressively, maybe it would've given her some answers, but she knew this wasn't the place to make enemies. Every Warden had the power of a clan behind them and they wouldn't take kindly to being accused of theft.

They weren't even obligated to talk to her, unless they were ordered from above. A delicate matter indeed, Sam thought.

"Everything alright?" Aaron asked as she joined him at the back of the class.

"Yes, I just needed some tips for Shadow,"

Samantha lied. The man seemed nice, but she couldn't trust him with her real problem. Not when everyone was a suspect.

She just had to figure this out before Lilith barged in the next day and disrupted the entire—

The class door swung open and a familiar head popped around the corner. *Lilith.*

CHAPTER SEVEN

"WHAT ARE YOU DOING HERE?" Sam hissed as she pulled the beautiful woman into the hallway, away from curious ears. "I thought you were leaving."

"I was, but then I changed my mind." Lilith looped her arm through Samantha's, the gesture strangely demanding and intimate at the same time. "I want to talk to the headmaster and you're coming with me."

"I'm... I'm in the middle of class," Sam protested, glaring at the Nox. Lilith Fatuus was a frightening woman when she wanted to be. Her cold, ice-blue eyes, the confidence in her voice, the posture of a fighter. Still, that didn't stop Sam from standing up to her. If she just gave in to every whim of the Nox, well... She didn't want to think about what kind of chaos that would cause.

"Take a break." She tugged on Sam's arm again. "Come on."

"But— Shadow..."

"Demon Bite can take care of herself."

Sam sighed. "I wish you'd stop calling her that. You'll confuse her."

"Nonsense. Hellhounds are a bit... Well, you know. Not the brightest."

"Hey!" Sam gasped, ignoring the memory of Shadow running into the wall. "You take that back."

Lilith's blue eyes shimmered like the brightest gems. "I won't and you can't make me."

"You're incorrigible."

"Why, thank you."

Half-bemused, half-irritated, Sam allowed the other woman to pull her to the headmaster's office. From experience, she knew that Lilith would do whatever she wanted to do. As long as she could temper the Nox, she counted that as a win.

* * *

THE BIG CLOCK in the headmaster's office ticked loudly as Samantha and Lilith sat on the leather bucket chairs, like two naughty children called to detention.

The elderly man sighed. "I did not expect to deal with someone of your stature today, Miss Fatuus."

Lilith's jaw clicked. "Someone stole my ring, my clan ring. I want the thief found and persecuted immediately. Fired, expelled, whatever power you have."

"I sure would love to help you, Miss Fatuus. Unfortunately, I hold no authority over any of the Wardens. I just run the facility."

"But—"

"Surely, you understand. Over the years, your father has made good use of the diplomatic qualities of the Wardens."

"What are you implying?" Lilith hissed.

"He's not implying anything," Samantha quickly interjected. She placed a hand on the other woman's arm, hoping to steady her. "Headmaster Eldridge, we just want to identify the thief and get the ring back. I promise the legality of the matter will be settled between the two clans, away from the Academy. We just need your help."

The man hesitated for a moment before sighing. "Alright, fine. I'll tell you what I can."

"Thank you."

"Five reports of stolen goods have been made to me in the past two months. No recent incidents though."

"Five?" Samantha echoed.

"Yes." He pulled a file from his drawer and presented her with a sheet of paper. "I can't disclose their names, but this is what went missing. Two bracelets, a necklace, a brooch, and another ring."

"Hmm… Interesting…" She studied the descriptions of the items in question before turning back to Lilith. "What material is your ring made from?"

"Silver, of course. The set gems are sapphires passed down for generations. Extremely valuable."

Samantha frowned. "All the other items on the list are silver too, but something doesn't add up. Lilith's ring is expensive, but this woman described her bracelet as having mostly sentimental value. So did the necklace owner. If it was just one item, sure… But this is too much of a coincidence. It almost feels like a personal matter. Do all these people have something in common?"

"I don't know." Eldridge muttered. He pulled the paper back and ran his finger down the list. "Not that I can think of…"

"They're not from the same clan? Same circles? What about overlapping time schedules?"

The man shook his head. "I don't know, we haven't had any incidents before those."

"Strange… What changed two months ago?"

"Nothing. Not that comes to mind... We put in new floors?"

Samantha sighed as she rose from the chair, her disappointment hidden behind a polite smile. "Thank you."

"Thank you?" Lilith echoed. "For what?"

"For his time." She pulled the other woman with her, hoping Lilith understood her glare. This was not the place to stir up trouble.

It wasn't until they were almost out of the door before the headmaster spoke again.

"Now that I think of it... Something else did happen back then. I usually wouldn't disclose this to outsiders, but since she's part of your clan... The receptionist made a complaint."

That certainly caught Samantha's attention. "A complaint? About what?"

"She... She accused another faculty member of harassment."

"Really?" Sam exchanged a look with Lilith. "Who was involved?"

"Susie, the receptionist. I can't tell you the other person who was involved though."

"That's fine, let's have a chat with her," Lilith declared. With a short nod, she acknowledged the headmaster and pulled Samantha along her warpath.

The empty halls echoed with the decisive clicks of her heels and Sam's thudding shoes.

They arrived at the reception, where Susie was sat behind her ancient computer. She blew a pink bubble with her chewing gum as she lazily clacked her long nails on the old keyboard. As soon as she saw Samantha and Lilith approach, she perked up.

"Miss Fatuus! What can I do for you today?" Her usually sharp voice lowered to an adoring, soft purr.

Samantha's stomach clenched in jealousy, but she didn't say anything. Lilith had made her opinion on human-Nox relationships crystal clear in the past. Humans were just for fun and that just wasn't enough for Sam.

"Two months ago, you filed a harassment claim with the headmaster," Lilith said, drumming her long fingers on the wooden desk. "What can you tell me about it?"

"Oh, that." Susie rolled her big eyes dramatically. "Just a little spat between colleagues, I don't want to talk about it. No, you're far more interesting to me. Do you know how rare it is for a member of the head family to visit a Warden facility? My gosh."

From the looks of it, Lilith seemed a bit taken aback and she sought out Samantha's eyes for reassurance. The latter just frowned, unsure of how to behave in the presence of another Warden. One that had been in the IF family for a lot longer than her.

"It's such an honour to meet you in person. They say you're so much like your father, but he would never have bothered to come here. Oh, what a delight."

"Susie, the harassment?" Lilith said, sounding a little exhausted.

"Oh, of course. *That*. It was really silly, obviously. I had a disagreement with a trainer. We had words, there might have been some light shoving, but she yanked on my hair." Susie smoothed her beautiful hair. "Do you know how long this takes to accomplish in the morning?"

Samantha frowned. She was beautiful, but she didn't seem too switched on.

"What did you two fight about? Did she steal something from you or something?" she asked, angling for something. Anything. She feared what Lilith would do if they couldn't find her ring and the culprit.

The receptionist cackled. "Goodness, no. About a month ago, the floors were being redone, and one of the builders was absolutely delicious. Since I arranged the renovation, she wanted me to give her his details, but I refused."

Lilith frowned. "Why?"

Susie played with her hair again. "Because."

"You wanted him for yourself," Samantha reasoned. The guilty look from the receptionist told her everything she needed to know. "That's what you two fought about?"

"She deserved it. She kept bugging me and one morning, I found her going through my computer. I talk to my mother on here, you know? I don't want someone else reading those conversations."

Samantha sighed. There was so much wrong with that, but she didn't even know where to start. She just tapped her hand on the desk, her own IF ring clacking against the wood. "Thanks."

"You're welcome. Oh, be careful with that ring," Susie said, pointing to Samantha's hand. "Things have a tendency to go missing around here."

"What? Why didn't you mention that before?!" Sam exclaimed. She barely managed to hold Lilith back, but she had to admit, she understood her frustration.

The receptionist shrugged. "You didn't ask."

Samantha took a deep, calming breath. "Okay. Tell me more about that."

"Well, first, it was Balthazar. He's really clumsy, so we just thought he misplaced his bracelet. But then more things started going missing, always jewelry. Tina, the kitchen lady, her necklace went missing yesterday."

"Yesterday?" Samantha echoed, turning to Lilith. "The headmaster said there were no recent reports."

"Oh, Tina didn't report it." The receptionist pulled a pink nail file from under a stack of papers and started filing.

That made no sense, Sam thought. "Why not?"

"Well…" Susie leaned across the desk, her voice reduced to a conspiratorial whisper. "It seemed silly to report the thefts to the thief."

That took Sam aback. "Are you implying the headmaster has been stealing from all of you?"

"Yes! Before he arrived, everything was fine. But three months ago, he showed up as the new principal and things started going missing! We put one and one together and poof. There you have it. We can't accuse him, of course. Not without losing our jobs."

The receptionist rattled on, but Samantha was no longer listening. She exchanged a worried look with Lilith, reassured to find the same concern in the Nox' eyes. This delicate matter just became even more delicate.

CHAPTER EIGHT

"Headmaster!"

Samantha and Lilith managed to catch the elderly man as he exited his office.

He turned around, the handle of his briefcase shrieking softly. "You two again?"

"We have to talk to you," Samantha said.

Eldridge sighed, his wrinkled forehead wrinkling even more. "Can't this wait until morning? I'm on my way home."

"Why didn't you tell us you've only been at the Academy for three months?" Lilith interjected.

"I didn't think it was relevant," he replied, back in motion.

"Not relevant? The thefts only started two months ago."

"I resent what you're insinuating, Miss Fatuus."

His voice was soft, but it held a quality that demanded respect. It didn't surprise Sam that he became the principal of this institute. It also meant he wouldn't take kindly to an accusation.

"We weren't insinuating anything," she hastily said, shooting Lilith an apologetic look. She usually wouldn't speak for the Nox, but this was a diplomatic matter. "We're just following every lead."

The older man scoffed. "Lead. Is that what you call rumours these days?"

Samantha didn't manage to keep the surprise of her face and from the headmaster's reaction, he noticed it.

"You don't think I know what's going on in my school?" He grimaced as they reached the double doors leading to the reception. They crossed the marble floor and followed the elderly man outside.

"Yet, you know nothing about all the thefts?" Lilith questioned, earning another glare from the man.

"Miss Fatuus, I sympathise with your cause and I've allowed you to question my staff. But this is neutral ground and you have no jurisdiction beyond what I grant you. You'd do well to remember that, especially when you insult my integrity."

Lilith's expression changed, her eyebrows knitting together in a dark frown. "And you'd do well to remember who I am."

"Lilith…" Sam hadn't meant to sound so pleading, but she was well aware of the bridges that had been built between the clans. If Lilith kept thundering through the Academy like a bull in a china shop, those bridges would soon go up in flames.

From the look on her face, Sam could tell Lilith wasn't here to take prisoners. She fiddled with her own ring, remembering the day Lilith gave it to her. She was attached to the little silver band and while she could relate to the grief of losing it, there was much more at stake here.

The two women locked eyes and Sam tried again. "Please?"

"Fine. My apologies, Headmaster." She shot him a polite smile, one that could fool an idiot.

The headmaster was no idiot. He sighed deeply and shook his greying head. "I'm going home and the Academy is closing soon. Goodbye."

The cold ground crackled as he walked away and left Samantha and Lilith with as few clues as when they started their investigation. The two women looked at each other, defeat sinking in.

"What do we do now?" Samantha asked.

"What I planned in the first place," the Nox replied, balls of light dancing in her eyes. "I'll turn this entire faculty upside down and question every living soul until I have my ring back."

Samantha sighed. "Right, any other plans *besides* declaring war?"

"Are you mocking me?"

"Yes, I am." She placed her hand on Lilith's lower arm, hoping to soften what she was going to say next. "I know you're attached to your ring, but it's unlikely we'll discover who took it."

"Do you hear yourself? This ring is always given to the Boss' successor. It's been in my family for centuries. I can't return without it."

"And do you hear yourself? You can't solve this with violence!" Samantha exclaimed, her temper flaring. "Eldridge is right, this is neutral territory. You can't just charge in."

The other woman pulled a face. "Well, your method isn't exactly working."

"Give me some time. Tomorrow is another day and I will figure this out, I promise." She drew Lilith's gaze up so they could lock eyes. Samantha softened as she recognised Lilith's distress and she resisted the urge to pull the other woman in a hug. Lilith had to be exhausted from always being tough and hard, even when she looked like she just wanted to cry.

Of course, Sam would never tell her that. She

might end up murdered herself for even suggesting Lilith was capable of vulnerability.

Instead, she squeezed the other woman's hand. "I promise we'll find your ring. Do you trust me?"

A brief moment of tension flickered between the two of them before a smile tugged on Lilith's lips and she finally nodded. "I do."

"Good. Can we go now?"

"Sure. Let's grab Demon Bite."

Samantha contained a chuckle. "Her name is Shadow."

"Demon Bite suits her better."

"It doesn't. It's a ridiculous name."

"Then you shouldn't have taken so long to name her," Lilith teased.

With a hidden smile, Sam followed her back into the Academy. She knew there was only one person that got to experience Lilith's playful side and she felt blessed it was her. She just wished it could be more than innocent jokes and stolen sweet moments between two work partners.

She stared at the Nox woman, mesmerised by the silky river of cascading hair and the brightest eyes she'd ever seen. She was a beauty to behold and a force of nature. Perhaps if this was a different world or a different life...

"You coming?" Lilith stared at Sam, her blue eyes

twinkling with something they only held when she looked at her.

Samantha shook the tempting thoughts out of her head and caught up. The other woman shot her a strange look.

"Everything alright?"

Samantha nodded. "Everything's peachy."

"Are you sure? You look like you had something serious on your mind."

If only she knew, Sam thought. Not ready for their relationship to change, or fall apart, Sam shrugged. "Nothing important. Just thinking about a cold beer."

"Of course," Lilith laughed. "After we pick up Demon Bite, we can go to the Drunken Turnip for a drink. My treat."

Sam hesitated for a moment, but that doubt was carried away when she saw how excited Shadow greeted Lilith and how she scratched the puppy's belly. For someone that claimed she didn't like hell-hounds, Lilith certainly had a lot of affection for her.

Maybe it was delusional, but Sam wanted to believe it was because who Shadow belonged to. That it mattered to the Nox that this was her puppy.

She turned to Lilith, caging a turmoil of feelings in her chest. "One drink."

CHAPTER NINE

THE DRUNKEN TURNIP was cosily crowded like always. Most customers greeted Lilith with a respectful nod or a well-meant grunt of acknowledgement. None of them bothered to greet Sam, but she didn't mind.

The beer was cold and the company…

She stared at Lilith and her stomach twisted in all kinds of knots and turns.

The company was something.

"A Whisp Hopper and a glass of wine. A big one," Lilith ordered before Samantha even had a chance to sit down.

She didn't particularly like being ordered for, but she would've been a lot more annoyed if it wasn't exactly what she wanted.

As she took a seat at the bar, Shadow strained against her lead and barked loudly.

"Wraf! Wraf!"

"Hey, what's going on?" Sam tried to distract the puppy by snapping her fingers and dancing her hands in front of the hellhound.

"Wraf! Grrrrr."

"Yikes, moody," Lilith remarked. She called after the bartender. "Bring a sausage for the dog."

The bartender nodded and returned with the drinks and a piece of sausage. The glasses were placed on the cardboard coasters with the Drunken Turnip logo and Sam gave a piece of sausage to Shadow, which she instantly devoured.

"Awr?"

She fed the puppy the rest of the meat, which seemed to settle her and with a satisfied hum, the hellhound laid down.

Lilith chuckled. "Aww, she was just hungry."

Samantha snorted. "She's always hungry. You should see her hoover up the crumbs in the morning."

"Adorable."

"I thought you didn't like hellhounds?"

The Nox's cheeks grew a little pinker. "I don't."

"You're very affectionate with Shadow," Samantha teased.

"Shut up."

A smile curled around Sam's lips. The great, eloquent and literate Lilith reduced to middle grade remarks. What a delight.

With a cold beer in hand and a satisfied pup curled around her ankles, Sam was enjoying the moment. She wasn't used to having much time off, but it was good for her. For both of them. Lilith had become a good influence on her life, even if she would never admit that out loud. Especially not to her.

"I'm sorry about your... you know," she said, gesturing to Lilith's hand.

"Don't be. I'll find the culprit and they'll wish they'd never met me."

"So... Like pretty much anyone you met?" she teased.

The other woman turned to look at her, a strange glance flickering through her eyes. "Do you feel that way?"

The intensity of Lilith's gaze had Samantha bat her eyes down. "No, I don't."

"Hmmm..."

The moment was ruined by a loud banging and Lilith whipped her hair back. "What's that noise?"

"I don't know."

Lilith gestured to the bartender. "Hey. What's that noise?"

The young guy swung his raggy towel over his shoulder and polished a wine glass. "Oh, that's just in the back. We're redoing the floors."

"Oh, right." Lilith nodded. "I forgot that started today. How is it going?"

"Not bad. They started really early, tore out all the wood and part of the marble floors."

"How long until it will be finished?" she asked while taking a sip from her rosé.

"Don't know. They found a nest of lunar rascals in the supply closet. Can you imagine? Bunch of those critters living here, stealing all our metal bottle caps and coins."

"Lunar rascals," Samantha echoed. "Aren't those small rodents?"

The bartender shrugged. "Yeah, so?"

"What did you say about the bottle caps and coins?"

"Oh, they like metal. They use it for their nests and to decorate themselves with it. Annoying little creatures. Don't know what they're doing here."

Sam snapped her fingers, trying to get the words to leave her mouth. "That, that's it! Lunar rascals!"

Lilith looked at her like she was crazy. "What?"

"These rodents are known for being handy little thieves, right?"

"Right…" It took a moment for things to dawn on Lilith. Her mouth fell open and she tripped over her own words, just like Sam. "Wait! You think…?"

"Yes, I think so! When they installed the floors two months ago, the Academy must've become home to a nest of lunar rascals. It fits, except… Don't they usually travel with Moon Hares?"

"Moon Hares," Lilith echoed softly. "The headmaster is a Moon Hare."

Samantha frowned. "He is? He's not a Warden?"

"No, he's Nox. You can tell from the colour of his skin and his small eyes. Definitely a Moon Hare from clan Lunatrix."

"He must've somehow attracted them." Sam downed the majority of her beer and wiped the cold moustache of foam away. "Let's go!"

"What? Now? I'm still drinking my wine"

"Are you serious? You've been whining about that ring all day." She tugged Lilith off her chair.

"Fine." The other woman downed her rosé and slipped off the stool. "The Academy is massive though. How are we going to find them?"

Sam glanced at her hellhound puppy, remembering her behaviour. A triumphant glow spread through from her stomach. "I know exactly where they are."

* * *

"Here." Sam reached the end of the corridor where she'd had her morning class and tapped her foot against a floorboard, reassured by the hollow sound. "This is it."

Lilith stared at her like she was crazy, but Sam wouldn't let that stop her. This was exactly where Shadow had barked that morning. The lunar rascal nest *had* to be there.

"Did you really have to call me here for that?" Susie asked, yawning demonstratively. "I'm missing the Lucky Wheel finale. Can't this wait until morning?"

"No." Lilith glared at her, her blue eyes shimmering dangerously. "You should be honoured to serve your clan."

"Oh, I am, but they've been building up to this episode for weeks now. Billy can stand to win—"

"Can you just shut up for five minutes?" Samantha quipped. "I'm trying to hear something."

The receptionist zipped her mouth with a ring-covered hand. "Sorry."

Sam knocked her boots against more boards,

until she was satisfied she found the right one. "Here, this one. Let's open it up. Lilith, hand me the axe."

The Nox woman snorted. "Does it look like I have an axe anywhere on me? Look at me, where would I be hiding it? In my—"

"Don't finish that sentence," Sam warned her. She hid her face, trying to get rid of the thoughts Lilith planted, and gestured to the red box on the wall. "I meant the fire axe."

"Oh."

The look on Lilith's face was one in a million and Sam adored it.

Lilith handed her the red axe, her cheeks still partially flushed. "Why didn't you just say so?"

"This was a lot funnier," Sam teased. She swung the axe back and rammed it between the thin gap where the floor met the wall. They weren't supposed to be used for anything but emergencies, but she was confident Lilith would argue this was in fact, an emergency.

"What are you doing?" a voice shouted. "Stop!"

Sam looked up to find the headmaster hurry toward them. She frowned and glared at the receptionist. "Why is he here? Did you tell him?"

"No, of course not!" Susie protested.

"I have an alert set for when the doors of the

school are opened after closing," Eldridge explained. He gestured to the red axe. "Now, put that down. I understand we got off on the wrong foot, but that's no reason to destroy this academy."

"Destroy?" It took Sam a moment to put two and two together and she lowered the axe. "Oh, no. I'm just tearing out the floor."

"Tearing out the floor?" The headmaster's hands flew into his greying hair. "We only put new ones in!"

Samantha nodded. "Exactly. We think that's when the school became home to a nest of lunar rascals. We thought that would interest you as, you know."

"Lunar rascals?" The man perked up so much, his ears wobbled. "Here? In the school? Give me the axe."

What a turn around, Samantha thought. She handed Headmaster Eldridge the red fire axe and he immediately swung it down. If he was the one destroying the floor, at least she wouldn't be liable for any damages.

She watched the older man strip the floor away, plank by plank, exposing the frame structure. The dusty underneath revealed clumps of dirt, some lost dog toys, and a bunch of other crap. None that indicated the presence of a lunar rascal nest though.

The bigger the gap grew, the more Samantha started doubting herself. Maybe they'd been wrong. Lunar rascals were rare and the Academy was really big. Maybe she'd come to the wrong conclusion after all.

"Anything?" She winced as yet another plank revealed more dust.

"What are you looking for again?" Susie asked as she inspected her red nails.

"Lunar rascals," Eldridge muttered, feverishly opening up the floor.

"Maybe there are none," Lilith suggested carefully.

The odds they would find a nest dwindled with every moment, but the headmaster didn't seem ready to accept it. Samantha's concern grew as she looked at the massive hole in the floor. The hallway was almost completely opened up and no rascals to show for it. If they didn't find the rodents, they were back to square one.

"Headmaster, maybe we made a mistake," Samantha admitted.

"No!" He rammed the axe into the floor again. "I want to find the rascals."

"There might be none…"

He wiped a bead of sweat from his face. The axe

thudded down, the vibrations amplified by the empty corridor. "But… No rascals?"

"It was just a theory. It looks like we were—" she paused. "Did you hear that?"

"What?"

"Shh-shh. I can hear something."

A soft, crittery chirp sounded from the floor and sure enough, as the headmaster peeled one more plank away, it exposed the nest. Two medium-sized rascals with big teeth and a long tail shrieked from the sudden light. One of them was seated on a pile of stolen jewels, the other had a necklace wrapped around its body. The two rascals scurried away with a chitter, abandoning their nest and leaving their looted treasures.

Sam bent down and fished a silver ring from the pile. "Gotcha."

EPILOGUE

BACK AT THE DRUNKEN TURNIP, Sam and Lilith clinked their glasses together in a well-deserved toast. The warm glow of the big lamps cast a sparkle on Lilith's hand and framed her signature silver ring beautifully.

All was well again.

Lilith shot her a dazzling smile. "To you."

"And you," Sam replied, shooting her a smirk of her own.

"Me? For what."

"For not starting a war," she teased.

Her friend rolled her blue eyes. "Oh, shush, you. We can't all be diplomatic geniuses and great finders. How did you even know that's where the rascals would be hiding?"

"Shadow feverishly barked at that spot when we arrived. And you thought hellhounds were useless." Sam sipped from her cold beer, savouring the bitter taste of the hop. It really was the perfect brew after a hard day of work.

"I stand corrected." She tore a piece from the dried sausage and held it up. "Here, Demon Bite. You want some?"

The puppy uncurled herself and wagged her tail excitedly. "Wraf!"

"Sit."

To Sam's surprise, the hellhound obeyed and earned herself a well-deserved piece of meat.

Lilith shot her a triumphant smile. "See, her name might actually *be* Demon Bite."

"Incorrigible." Another smile curled around Sam's lips. Some things just never changed and she really hoped they wouldn't. She fiddled with her own ring, twirling the band around her finger. "What will happen to the lunar rascals?"

"Lunar rascals are sacred to Moon Hares. Headmaster Eldridge will give them a good home," Lilith said as she sipped her wine. "Ahh, what a day."

Samantha smiled. She was impressed with Lilith and how despite her anger and frustration, she'd never taken it out on anyone. She hadn't used her magic or bent someone's will. She'd followed the rules, even though she was the one that could rewrite them.

Lilith realised Sam was staring at her and frowned. "What?"

"Nothing," Sam lied, casting her gaze back down. She couldn't tell Lilith this, not without realising something she'd been trying to ignore for a while now.

"You sure? You're staring at me."

"I was thinking about the receptionist," Sam deflected.

"Yeah? What about her?"

"She was just so..." She searched for the right word. A kind word. "Incompetent."

Lilith snorted. "Oh, she was horrible."

"How did she even become a Warden? I thought the clans always carefully selected which humans to bring into the Nox. Even you thought about it, although we both know what you did was really unethical."

"I guess my father and I have similar taste then," Lilith teased.

A gasp escaped Sam. "Oh! Are you saying I'm incompetent too? I found your ring."

"No, I meant beautiful."

A blush crept up Sam's neck and settled on her cheeks. She knew how to handle Lilith's teasings, but compliments? That was a lot harder. She wasn't used to people speaking kindly of her or to her.

Lost for words, she sipped from her beer to bridge the not-uncomfortable silence. An ambient atmosphere always hung in the Drunken Turnip and the soft chatter and occasional clatters added a strange softness to the world around her.

When she dared look at Lilith again, she found the woman already staring at her. Her piercing blue eyes caught hers in a surprisingly vulnerable gaze.

"I know it was messed up what I did. Do you regret it?"

"I don't know." Sam sighed, and as she looked at the Nox, she softened with affection. Lilith had tricked her into joining the supernatural world and for a long time, she resisted it. But the longer she was part of it all, the more she realised something. She'd finally found a place where she mattered.

She locked eyes with Lilith, mesmerised by her beautiful blues as always. "No, I don't regret it."

"Me either," Lilith admitted softly. She heaved her glass again. "Another toast. To more adventures?"

A smile tugged on Samantha's lips. "To a lot more adventures."

— *The End (but not really)* —

Read more about Samantha, Lilith, and Shadow in The Case Of The Night Mark, a full-sized novel where the three characters meet and Sam gets her first taste of the Nox world. She'll have another mystery to solve that will turn her life upside down.

https://books2read.com/thenightmark

If you're loving academies and want to read more about that, you should check out Valkyrie 101. It's a different world, but with just as much magic and adventure. Who doesn't want to learn how to become a Valkyrie?

https://books2read.com/valkyrie101

Thank you for getting this book and I hope you've enjoyed it! See you in the next one. — Ari

ALSO BY ARIZONA TAPE

The Samantha Rain Mysteries (urban fantasy f/f)

1. The Case Of The Night Mark
2. The Case Of the Pixie Deal
3. The Case Of The Ruby Curse

- The Case Of The Puppy Academy

The Afterlife Academy: Valkyrie (urban fantasy academy f/f)

1. Valkyrie 101 (also in audio)
2. Valkyrie 102
3. Valkyrie 103
4. Valkyrie 104
5. Valkyrie 105
6. Valkyrie 106
7. Valkyrie 107

- Wings of Grief

The Griffin Sanctuary (modern fantasy f/f)

1. The Unicorn Herd

The Heir Of The East (completed paranormal academy f/f)

1. Valkyrie's Oath
2. Valkyrie's Choice

My Winter Wolf Trilogy (completed paranormal fantasy f/f romance)

1. Wolf's Whisper (also in audio)
2. Wolf's Echo
3. Wolf's Howl
4. A Squad Of Wolves (Danny's Story)

- White Wolf, Black Wolf (Short Story Prequel)
- My Winter Wolf Trilogy Boxed Set

Rainbow Central (new adult f/f romance)

- Love Is For Later
- New Lease Of Love
- Please Be My Love
- Love For The Holidays

The Romance Projects (contemporary)

- Project Crush

My Own Human Duology (completed paranormal dystopian f/f romance)

1. My Own Human
2. Your Own Human

- My Own Human Boxed Set

Twisted Trilogy (dark contemporary f/f romance)

1. Play To Kiss (also in audio)
2. Play To Kill (also in audio)
3. Play To Keep

Grimm's Dweller Trilogy (completed fantasy fairy tale retelling)

1. Bittersweet Beginning
2. Bittersweet Journey
3. Bittersweet Ending

- Grimm's Dweller Trilogy boxed set

Standalone Contemporary Titles

- The Love Pill (f/f)
- Four Gamers and Me (Poly with f/f)
- Choosing Her Boxed Set

Standalone Fantasy

- Beyond the Northern Lights

Twin Souls Trilogy, co-written with Laura Greenwood
(completed paranormal romance)

1. Soulswap (also in audio)
2. Soulshift (also in audio)
3. Soultrade (also in audio)

- Twins Souls Boxed Set (also in audio)

Dragon Soul Series, co-written with Laura Greenwood
(paranormal romance)

1. Dragon Destiny
2. Dragon Heart
3. Dragon Outcast (Audiobook Available)

Renegade Dragons, co-written with Laura Greenwood
(completed paranormal romance)

1. Fifth Soul (also in audio)
2. Fifth Round (also in audio)
3. Fifth Flame (also in audio)

- Renegade Dragons Boxed Set (also in audio)

Partridge In The Pear, co-written with Skye MacKinnon
(sci-fi romance)

ABOUT THE AUTHOR

A creator at heart, Ari has always been in love with the idea of turning nothing into something. With her rainbow bat familiar, Sprinkles, she's ready to conquer the book world. Whether it's dragons and vampires or princesses and students, she always knows where to find the romance.

FOLLOW THE AUTHOR

- Website: www.arizonatape.com
- Mailing List: www.arizonatape.com/subscribe
- Facebook Page: http://facebook.com/arizonatapeauthor
- Reader Group: http://facebook.com/groups/arizonatape
- Bookbub: http://www.bookbub.com/authors/arizona-tape
- Instagram: http://instagram.com/arizonatape

Printed in Great Britain
by Amazon